ISBN 0-86163-689-9

This edition first published 1993
Third impression 1999

Published by Award Publications Limited,
27 Longford Street, London NW1 3DZ

Printed in Singapore

BRER RABBIT STORIES

Illustrated by RENE CLOKE

AWARD PUBLICATIONS LIMITED

BRER FOX AND MRS GOOSE

Mrs Goose was down by the water doing her washing one day when Brer Fox passed along on the other side of the river.

"Ha, ha!" he muttered. "That nice fat goose would make me a very tasty supper. I'll creep into her house tonight when she is asleep and catch her."

He didn't know that Brer Rabbit was listening to his plan but, as soon as the fox was out of sight, Brer Rabbit hopped over the stepping-stones to warn Mrs Goose.

"What shall I do?" wailed Mrs Goose in a great flutter. "I can't escape from that dreadful Brer Fox if he breaks into my house," and she cried and cried and made her washing wetter and wetter.

"Just listen to me," said Brer Rabbit, who was always ready to play tricks on Brer Fox, "make a bundle of your washing and put it in your bed, then fly up to the rafters and roost there for the night. I'll have a chat with Brer Dog, he will help you."

So that night, Mrs Goose did as Brer Rabbit had advised.

She made a big bundle of her washing and put it in her bed in a dark corner then she flew up to the rafters and waited rather nervously to see what would happen.

Sure enough, at midnight, the door opened softly and Brer Fox crept in.

The room was so dark that it was easy to mistake the bundle of washing for a fine fat goose and Brer Fox, licking his lips, grabbed it and rushed out.

But Brer Dog was waiting for him, and if the fox hadn't dropped the bundle and run for his life, he would certainly have been caught.

The next morning the story went around that Brer Fox had tried to steal Mrs Goose's washing!

All the animals laughed and laughed to think that the fine and cunning Brer Fox had wanted to steal anything so silly as Mrs Goose's washing!

THE MOON IN THE POND

One evening when all the animals were feeling friendly, they decided to go fishing together.

But when they reached the pond, Brer Rabbit looked very worried.

"Look!" he cried. "The moon has fallen into the water; we shan't catch any fish here until we have scooped it out."

So Brer Rabbit ran home to fetch a strong net.

"It seems to me," whispered Brer Fox, "that the moon is made of gold; I'm sure Brer Rabbit will try to keep it for himself so we mustn't let him get hold of it."

When Brer Rabbit came back with the net, Brer Fox took it from him.

"Let Brer Wolf and Brer Bear help me," he said, "you are too small to wade into the pond and pull that heavy moon from the water."

This was just what Brer Rabbit had planned so, while the big animals waded into the water, Brer Rabbit and his friend, Brer Tortoise, crept to the other side of the pond and started fishing.

Brer Fox, Brer Wolf and Brer Bear waded deeper and deeper into the water and tried to drag the net around the moon but, of course, as it was only the reflection of the moon, they couldn't catch it.

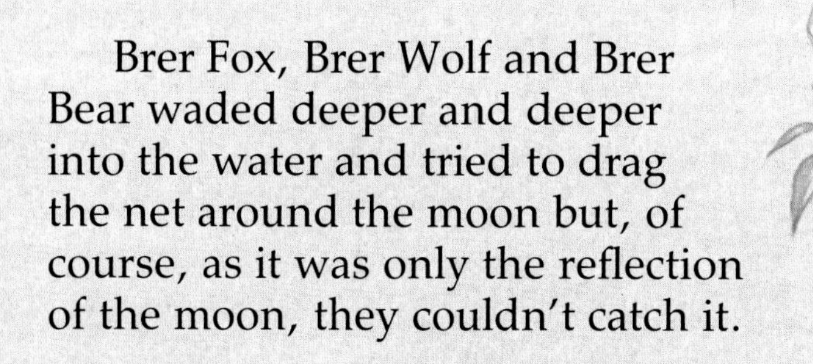

Then Brer Fox slipped and Brer Bear, stumbling over him, clutched Brer Wolf and they fell into the pond with a mighty splash!

When they had struggled back to the bank they saw Brer Rabbit and Brer Tortoise hurrying away with a basket of fine fish.

"Tricked again!" they growled.

BRER RABBIT AND THE HONEYPOT

Brer Rabbit was peeping through the grass one day when he saw Brer Bear walking down the road.

"I'll have a look inside Brer Bear's house," said the little rabbit, "there might be something nice to eat there."

He hopped along, and finding the door open, crept inside Brer Bear's house.

"Only bread and cheese on the table," grumbled Brer Rabbit. "I don't want that. I wonder what he keeps in the cupboard? Perhaps some lettuces or carrots or maybe a bag of oats."

Standing on a stool, Brer Rabbit opened the cupboard door.

"Nothing but cups and plates," muttered the rabbit, "except for that jar on the top shelf," and he stretched up a paw to reach it.

"O—oh!" over went the jar and out poured a stream of honey!

Poor Brer Rabbit was covered with sticky honey from head to foot, and although he licked and licked, it still stuck to him.

"Deary me!" he cried. "I like honey but not all over me! If I go out the bees will come after me and perhaps sting me if they think I've stolen their honey, and if I stay here Brer Bear will catch me."

At last he decided to run into the wood and roll in the leaves to rub off the honey.

This wasn't a very good idea for the leaves stuck to the honey and made Brer Rabbit look a terrifying person.

But when he saw that the other animals were frightened of him, he thought he might be able to scare his old enemy, Brer Fox, so he walked along waving his arms and making the leaves give a peculiar 'swishy' noise.

When Brer Bear saw him, he gave a howl and ran for his life and didn't stop until he was safely home.

The next animals Brer Rabbit met were Brer Fox and Brer Wolf.

They were busily making a plan to catch Brer Rabbit and didn't see him until he jumped onto a hillock in front of them.

“Gr—gr, I’m the Bogy Man!” shouted Brer Rabbit. “I eat bad wolves and foxes—I’ll catch you both!”

“Help!” howled Brer Wolf.
“Help!” barked Brer Fox, as Brer Rabbit shook his leaf—covered paws in the air—and off they ran!

It took Brer Rabbit a long time to clean off the honey but how he laughed! And every time he saw Brer Fox he shouted—
“Mind the Bogy Man doesn’t get you!”

BRER WOLF BREAKS THE LAW

As Brer Rabbit was walking along one day, he was thinking as usual of what tricks he could play on Brer Fox and Brer Wolf, but this time, he was nearly caught himself.

"Help! help!" came a voice from nearby and Brer Rabbit saw that Brer Wolf had been trapped under a great boulder.

"Please help me!" cried the wolf. "Give the boulder a push and set me free."

So Brer Rabbit, feeling rather sorry for the wolf although he didn't really like him, gave the boulder a mighty heave and out crawled Brer Wolf.

But instead of thanking Brer Rabbit, Brer Wolf seized him by the ears and declared he would have rabbit pie for dinner that night.

"That's a fine way to say thank you," squeaked Brer Rabbit, "I'll never do you a good turn again as long as I live!"

"You certainly won't!" laughed Brer Wolf.

Then Brer Rabbit thought quickly.

"Of course, you know, Brer Wolf that it's breaking the law to kill anyone who rescues you?" he said.

"No, I didn't know that," answered Brer Wolf, doubtfully.

"Well," said Brer Rabbit, "we must ask Brer Tortoise, he's the expert on these matters. There'll be trouble for you if you are proved wrong."

So Brer Wolf agreed to go to Brer Tortoise's house.

Brer Tortoise looked very wise when they asked for his opinion but, luckily, he was a friend of Brer Rabbit and wanted to help him.

"This is a very difficult case," he said at last when both animals had explained what had happened, "but we must be certain that the law isn't broken. Before I can decide, I must see the scene where this took place."

So off went the three animals.

Brer Tortoise poked the boulder and walked around it.

"There is only one way to decide," he said to Brer Wolf, "I must see just how you were trapped."

So Brer Wolf crawled under the boulder and the tortoise and the rabbit rolled it over him. Then Brer Tortoise said,

"Brer Rabbit, you were wrong. If you found Brer Wolf under that boulder he was minding his own business and you should have minded yours."

And Brer Tortoise and Brer Rabbit walked off and left Brer Wolf to be rescued by someone else.